LEVEL 2

# LEGO NINJAGO LEGACY

# BACK IN ACTION!

SCHOLASTIC INC.

ISBN: 978-1-338-58283-3

10 9 8 7 6 5 4 3 2 1          20 21 22 23 24

Printed in the U.S.A.          40

First printing 2020

Book design by Cheung Tai

"Ow! You just hit me, Kai!" Jay complained.

"Sorry, I thought you were the dummy," Kai said.

The ninja were blindfolded for a training exercise.

Cole laughed. "But he is the dummy."

"Very funny, Cole," Jay said.

Workers were rebuilding the Monastery of Spinjitzu around them as they trained. Not long ago, Garmadon had destroyed Ninjago City and the monastery—again.

"Master Wu, why are we wearing these blindfolds?" Lloyd asked.

Master Wu smiled. "This training allows you to sharpen your other senses," he said.

The ninja continued their training.

"Aaaaaayaaaa!!" Kai yelled. He lunged at a training dummy, whacking Jay by mistake.

Jay tumbled across the floor and bumped into a cart with wheels.

**Bam!** The cart crashed into a ladder. The ladder wobbled.

"Help!" cried the worker on the ladder.

Jay tore off his blindfold. He caught the falling worker.

Jay gazed at the splattered paint on himself. "I kind of like this look," he said.

Zane did not see the spilled paint. He slipped and slid across the floor!

***Bam!*** He slammed into a worker carrying a vase. The vase wobbled in his hands.

Nya caught the vase before it fell.

"Careful!" Master Wu scolded the ninja. "These workers are returning rare objects to the gallery."

"Um, maybe we shouldn't be training blindfolded if this stuff is so rare?" Cole asked.

"Maybe you should pay attention to the lesson I am teaching," Master Wu replied.

"You know, not too long ago *we* were the ones giving *you* lessons," Cole teased.

During a battle with the Time Twins, Master Wu had been turned into a baby. He grew up again quickly, becoming a boy, a teen, a man, and then an old man once again.

When Wu was growing up the second time, the ninja had helped train him.

"We all can learn from each other," Master Wu said. "Please put your blindfolds back on."

Before they could obey, their friend Dareth walked in.
He liked to call himself the Brown Ninja.

"Blindfolds? Are we playing a game?" he asked.

"Dareth, the ninja are training," Master Wu told him. "Got it!" Dareth cried. He took the sash off his pants and blindfolded himself with it.

"Hiii-yah!" he cried, doing a spinning kick.
"Dareth, please stop!" Master Wu said.

**Bam!** He kicked over a big glass case. It shattered.

"Whoops!" Dareth said. "Well, at least it was empty."

"That glass case was not empty," Master Wu said.
"It held six Invisible Ninja Squirrels. They are a rare
breed of Ninja Squirrels found here, in the Mountains
of Impossible Height."

"Invisible Ninja Squirrels?" Kai asked. "That's nuts!"

"Exactly," Zane said. "In the paws of a Ninja Squirrel, an acorn from these mountains can become an explosive Shurike-nut."

"But there were no nuts in the glass case," Cole pointed out.

"Correct," Master Wu said. "But squirrels have an uncanny ability to locate nuts they have buried. It is highly possible that . . ."

# BOOM!

"Those furry little ninja are going to destroy the monastery!" Jay cried.

"Not if we can help it," Lloyd said. "Ninja, let's capture the squirrels and save the monastery!"

The ninja let out a cheer. "Ninjaaaaago!"

Then they looked around the room.

"Okay, so how can we capture them if they're invisible?" Kai asked.

***Boom!*** A column exploded.

"Over there!" Nya yelled, pointing.

"Follow the explosions!" Master Wu ordered. "I will find another container that will hold them."
He ran off.

Jay ran toward the explosion. He swung at where the squirrel should have been, but it wasn't there.

"Come here, little squirrel," he said. Then . . . *POW!* An invisible squirrel kicked him.

"No fair!" Jay protested. "How can we catch something we can't see?"

"Perhaps, as Master Wu said, we should sharpen our other senses," Zane said.

"How can our other senses help us? The squirrels are invisible," Kai said.

"They are invisible, but they are not ghosts," Zane said. "They have solid bodies. I will zero in on their heat signatures," he said. "Target spotted!"

Zane revealed the heat coming from the squirrel's body. It made a glowing outline. The ninja quickly grabbed the creature.

"One down," Zane reported.

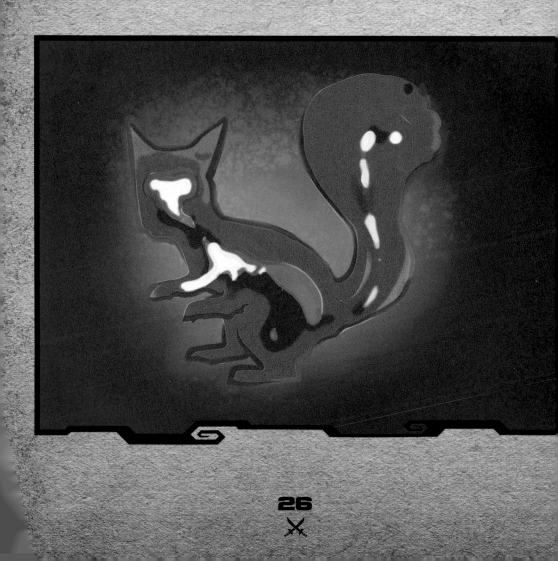

"I've got the next one!" Jay cried.

***Boom!*** One of the squirrels threw a Shurike-nut at a training dummy. Jay whizzed around. He sent a lightning blast flying to where the squirrel should have been.

A sizzling outline appeared around the squirrel! The creature ran, but Jay could see it now. He somersaulted across the room and scooped it up.

"Two down!" he cried.

"My turn!" Lloyd said. "With my powers, I can change the color of any energy field."

He waited for the next squirrel to make a move. **Boom!** Another statue exploded.

Lloyd aimed a blast of green energy at the statue. The squirrel's invisible force field started glowing green. Lloyd quickly captured the squirrel.

"I've got number four!" Nya cried. She sprayed a squirrel with water and followed the drips until she had it cornered.

"Smoke blast!" Kai yelled. The Ninja Squirrel began to cough.

"I can't see you, but I can hear you!" Kai cried. Then he captured the furry creature.

"I've got the last one!" Cole said.

**Boom!!** Cole heard the noise and spun around.
He sent a cloud of dirt flying at the squirrel.

"Gotcha!" Cole cried. "Ow! Quit biting, little guy!"

Master Wu came back with a new glass case.

"Quickly, get the Ninja Squirrels into this case!"

The ninja put the angry, chattering squirrels into the case.

"Good job, ninja," Master Wu said.

"You were right, Master Wu," Lloyd told him. "There are still things we can learn from you."

Master Wu grinned. "Now you are seeing clearly."